# SATURDAY

## IS SWIMMING DAY

JUNE

| S | M | T | W | T | F | S |
|---|---|---|---|---|---|---|
| | | | | | 1 | (2) |
| 3 | 4 | 5 | 6 | 7 | 8 | (9) |
| 10 | 11 | 12 | 13 | 14 | 15 | (16) |
| 17 | 18 | 19 | 20 | 21 | 22 | (23) |
| 24 | 25 | 26 | 27 | 28 | 29 | (30) |

*For Sahn*

First edition 2018

Library of Congress Catalog Card Number pending
ISBN 978-0-7636-9117-2

TLF 23 22 21 20 19 18
10 9 8 7 6 5 4 3 2 1

Printed in Dongguan, Guangdong, China

This book was typeset in Filosofia.
The illustrations were done in watercolor and colored pencil.

Candlewick Press
99 Dover Street
Somerville, Massachusetts 02144

visit us at www.candlewick.com

# SATURDAY
# IS SWIMMING DAY

## Hyewon Yum

CANDLEWICK PRESS

It was Saturday morning.
I told my mom that my stomach hurt.

She took my temperature
and said I didn't have a fever, so I could still go to
my swim lesson.

She rubbed my tummy and said that it would probably feel better once I got there.
I didn't think so.

Mom packed my strawberry bathing suit and my too-small swim cap.

When we got to the pool, Mom said, "This is Mary. She'll be teaching you. And I'll be waiting right outside when you're done. Have fun!"

LOCKER ROOM

I changed ever so slowly.

I even went to the bathroom three times.
When Mary called everyone to the pool,
I was the last in line.

The pool was loud, and the floor was slippery and cold.
My head felt tight inside my swim cap.
And my stomach still hurt.

When Mary whistled for the lesson to start,
some kids jumped right in and made big splashes.
Mary said it was OK not to get in if my stomach hurt.

I sat on the edge of the pool the whole time.
After class was over, my stomach felt better.

I took off my swim cap and showered
so my hair would be wet like everyone else's.

The next Saturday, I had a very bad stomachache.

WET
TOWELS

When Mary blew the whistle, I did not get in.
I told her I had a stomachache again, and she said
she would hold me so I could practice ice-cream
scoops like the other kids.

Mary helped me get into the pool.
The water was warm and made my
stomach feel a little better.

I did ice-cream scoops and kicks.

Then we crossed the whole pool.

That night, when I took a bath, I practiced my kicks.

The next Saturday, I didn't have a stomachache.
I packed my bathing suit and my new swim cap.

When we got to the pool, Mary blew the whistle
and I got into the water carefully.

Mary held my hands and I showed her my kicks.
She said they were very good.

Then Mary said to put floats on our stomachs
so we could be starfish.

She put her hands under me and helped me
lie back in the water.

It was so quiet with my ears in the water,
and everything looked different.

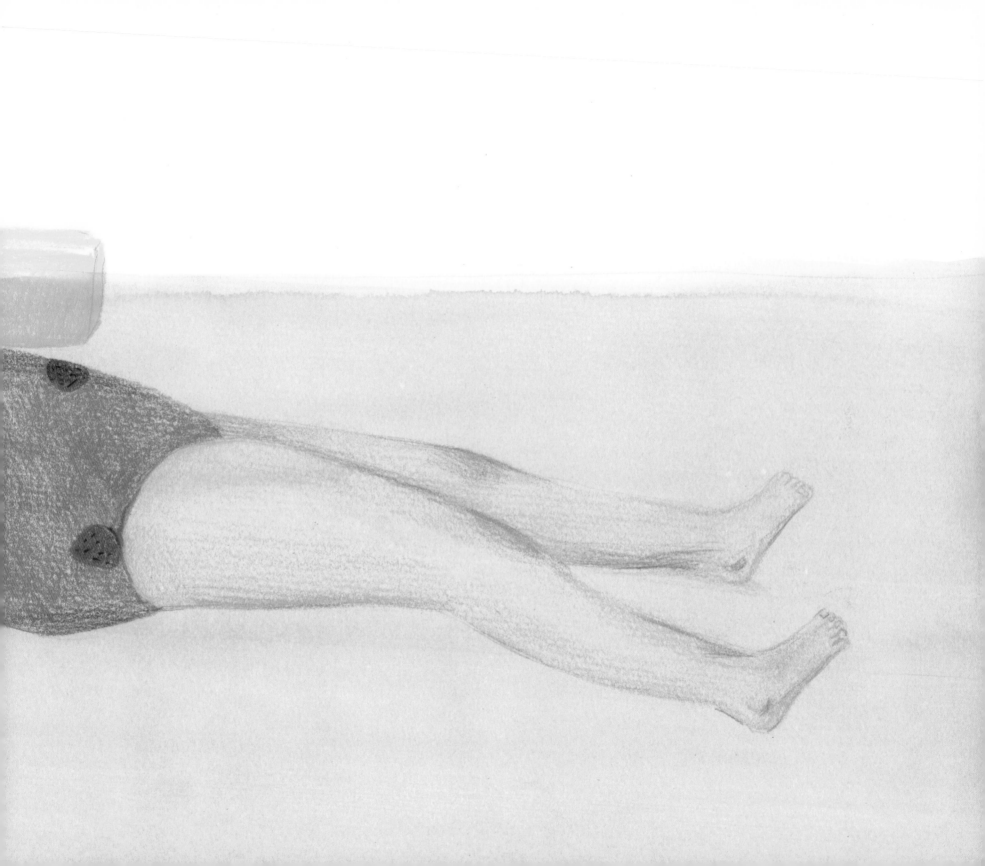

I wanted to tell Mary that I loved being a starfish,
but she wasn't holding me anymore.

She caught me right away.
I told her I was OK, so she
asked me if I wanted to try again.

First she stayed right next to me, and then I said she could let go.

I floated all by myself!

After starfish, we did kicking with friends to see who could make the biggest splashes.

I even did two bobs. Next week maybe I'll do ten bobs.

And no stomachache!